Happy Birthday
Mateo!

Love,
Evelyn & Eleanor

Take a deep breath
namaste ♪

D0944082

Yoga Adventure!

written and sung by
Jamaica Stevens and JAMaROO Kids

illustrated by Rocío Alejandro

Barefoot Books
step inside a story

Pretend to be a big **plane**! Fly across the sky. Look at all the clouds as we pass by.

Over seven continents and five oceans too,
Off we go together, learning something new!

Yoga adventure — where will it take you?

First stop is **North America**!

Move like a **bison** in a yoga pose.
Big and strong with warrior arms,

Let's feel our strength grow.

Pretend to ride a **bicycle**! Pedal very far.
Through the forest, past the trees —
quick, it's getting dark!

Through North America (and Central too!),
Off we go together, learning something new.

South America, me and you!

Roll like a **chinchilla**
in a yoga pose.

Rock side to side in the dust,
Moving fast then slow.

Now, let's go and explore **Europe**!

Stretch like a **grey wolf**
in a yoga pose.

Push your tail up to the sky
And breathe in through your nose.

Pretend to be a long **train** going down the tracks!
Chugging through the mountains, caboose is in the back.

Through many countries, chugga-choo-choo,
Off we go together, learning something new.

Next stop is **Asia**, me and you!

Sit like a **panda**
in a yoga pose.

Bend over to eat bamboo
With your panda toes.

Pretend to be a **sailboat** sailing fast and free!
Vast blue water, far as we can see.

Indian Ocean skies are blue.
   Off we go together, learning something new.

Here we come, **Australia**, me and you!

Rest like a **koala** in a yoga pose.
Raise your arms above your head
and off to sleep we'll doze.

Now, let's go to **Africa**!

Squat like a **clawed frog** in a yoga pose,
Ground your feet and push your knees
Out with your elbows.

Pretend to be a **submarine**
deep down in the sea!
Look at all the fish swimming playfully.

See the icebergs and fur seals too.
Off we go together, learning something new.

Now we're in **Antarctica**,
me and you!

Lie like a **baleen whale** in a yoga pose.
Use your arms to lift up high
And look at the rainbow.

Now it's time to slow down.
We've learned something new.

Let's lie down in Shavasana.
Our trip is through.

I'm feeling grateful for this time with you!

Explore the Yoga Poses!

* Yoga comes from ancient India, where people spoke Sanskrit. For each pose, you will find the name used in this book, the common English name and the original Sanskrit name.

* Yoga can be done inside or outside, at home or at school! You can do yoga alone or with family and friends.

* If you're outdoors, make sure you're on a soft surface, like grass. If you're indoors, find an open space so that you do not bump into furniture.

* Yoga mats are great, but if you do not have one, try using a large towel or a blanket instead. On a hard floor, place a rug beneath your towel or blanket so it does not slip.

Plane   *Warrior III Pose / Virabhadrasana III*

① Stand up tall, feet planted on the ground, toes facing forwards.

② Stretch your arms out on both sides to create plane wings.

③ Transfer your weight to your right leg and find balance.

④ Slowly lift your left leg behind you, keeping that leg straight while leaning forwards with your upper body.

⑤ Repeat on the left side.

Bison
Warrior II Pose / Virabhadrasana II

① Stand with your legs wide apart, toes facing forwards.

② Turn your right foot out to point sideways.

③ Bend your right knee, keeping your knee directly over your ankle. Keep your left leg straight.

④ Reach your arms out straight above your legs. Look out over your right hand.

⑤ Repeat on the left side.

Bicycle
Boat Pose Variation / Navasana Variation

① Sit up straight with your legs extended in front of you.

② Bend your knees and press your feet into the mat.

③ Lean back until you feel your tummy muscles tighten.

④ Reach your arms out in front of you like you are holding onto bike handles.

⑤ Lift your legs and pedal as if you are riding a bike.

⑥ A strap or band around your feet might help.

Chinchilla
Happy Baby Pose / Ananda Balasana

① Lie on your back and bring your knees in towards your chest.

② Grab the outsides of your feet and pull your legs wide apart.

③ Keeping your knees bent, press your feet into your hands. Try to keep your back pressed into the mat.

④ Gently rock from side to side, like a baby or a chinchilla.

Grey Wolf
Downward Dog Pose / Adho Mukha Svanasana

① Place your hands and knees on the mat. This is called tabletop position.

② Tuck your toes under, press your hands and feet into the mat, then straighten your arms and legs.

③ Push your hips up towards the sky. Your body should make a triangle shape like a mountain or a teepee.

Train
Staff Pose / Dandasana

① Sit up tall on your mat, legs straight out in front of you.

② Breathe in as you raise your arms up over your head with your palms facing each other.

③ As you breathe out, fold your upper body over your legs.

④ Move your arms in a circular motion like train wheels going down the tracks.

Panda
Butterfly Pose / Baddha Konasana

① Sit on the ground and press the bottoms of your feet together in front of you.

② Allow your knees to fall open towards the ground.

③ Hold onto your feet and sit up straight and tall.

④ Bend over to bring your nose down towards your toes.

Sailboat   *Boat Pose / Navasana*

① Sit up straight with your legs extended in front of you.

② Bend your knees and press your feet into the mat.

③ Lean back until you feel your tummy muscles tighten.

④ Reach your arms out in front of you with your palms facing one another.

⑤ ... slightly ...

Koala
Child's Pose / Balasana

① Start in tabletop position, hands and knees on the mat.

② Touch your toes together behind you.

③ Push your hips back towards your heels and let your upper body sink down towards the mat.

④ Press your palms down and let your forehead rest on the mat.

⑤ You can keep your knees apart so your belly can sink towards the mat or bring your knees together and rest your belly on your thighs.

Clawed Frog
Garland Pose / Malasana

① Stand with your feet apart, a bit wider than your hips.

② Turn your feet out at a 45-degree angle.

③ Slowly lower your bottom towards the ground until you land in a squat, like a frog. Try to keep your heels on the ground.

④ Bring your palms together and press your elbows into your inner knees.

Submarine
Bow Pose / Dhanurasana

① Lie on your belly, with your arms along your sides, palms facing down.

② Bend your knees and grab onto the outside of each ankle.

③ Breathe in and kick back with your heels. Lift your chest and head up to the sky so your body makes a basket or bowl shape.

Baleen Whale
Cobra Pose / Bhujangasana

① Lie on your belly.

② Bring your feet together so that your toes, ankles and knees touch.

③ Place your hands under your shoulders and pull your elbows in towards your sides.

④ Press your hands and the tops of your feet into the mat.

⑤ Straighten your arms, lift up your chest and look up to the sky.

Seated Pose / Sukhasana

① Sit up tall with a long, straight back. Imagine that you are reaching the top of your head towards the sky.

② Cross your legs like a pretzel.

③ Press your hands together in front of your heart.

Resting Pose / Shavasana

① Lie on your back with your feet shoulder distance apart.

② Place your arms by your sides with your palms facing up.

③ Take a deep breath and relax, letting your body melt into the floor.

④ If you want to, you can place your hands gently on your tummy. Feel it rise as you breathe in and fall as you breathe out.

Meet the Animals!

Bison (North America) can run up to 35 miles (56 km) per hour. That's as fast as a car! They are the largest land animal in North America.

A **grey wolf** (Europe) can eat 20 to 30 pounds (9 to 13 kg) of meat in one meal. That's about as much as three turkeys!

Arctic Ocean

EUROPE

ASIA

Pandas (Asia) spend about 12 hours a day eating!

NORTH AMERICA

Atlantic Ocean

Pacific Ocean

AFRICA

Chinchilla (South America) fur is extremely soft and thick. It protects them from the cold night air in the mountains where they live.

SOUTH AMERICA

Indian Ocean

AUSTRALIA

Southern Ocean

Koalas (Australia) spend up to 18 hours a day sleeping! They get very little energy from the eucalyptus leaves they eat.

ANTARCTICA

The **baleen whale** (Antarctica) has no teeth. It uses a comb-shaped part of its mouth, called a baleen, to trap tiny ocean creatures.

A **clawed frog** (Africa) can burrow in the mud and lie dormant — in a special kind of deep sleep — for up to a year.

Yoga Adventure!

♩ = 120

Pre - tend to be a big plane! Fly a-cross the sky. Look at all the clouds as we pass by.

O - ver se - ven con - tin - ents and five o - ceans too, Off we go to - ge - ther,

learn - ing some-thing new! Yo - ga ad-ven - ture— where will it take you? (First stop is North America!)

slower

Move like a bi - son in a yo - ga pose. Big and strong with war-rior arms, Let's feel our strength grow.

To all teachers and childcare providers: thank you for doing such important work in the world — J. S.

For Abril, David and Julián — R. A.

Barefoot Books, 23 Bradford Street, 2nd Floor, Concord, MA 01742
29/30 Fitzroy Square, London, W1T 6LQ

Text copyright © 2021 by Jamaica Stevens and JAMaROO Kids
Illustrations copyright © 2021 by Rocío Alejandro
The moral rights of Jamaica Stevens, JAMaROO Kids
and Rocío Alejandro have been asserted

Sung by Jamaica Stevens and JAMaROO Kids. Musical composition, arrangement
and recording copyright © ℗ 2021 by Jamaica Stevens and JAMaROO Kids
Recorded, mixed and mastered by Joel Jaffe at Studio D / World Studios
Animation by Collaborate Agency, UK

First published in the United States of America by Barefoot Books, Inc
and in Great Britain by Barefoot Books, Ltd in 2021. All rights reserved

Graphic design by Elizabeth Jayasekera, Barefoot Books
Edited and art directed by Lisa Rosinsky, Barefoot Books
Reproduction by Bright Arts, Hong Kong. Printed in China on 100% acid-free paper

This book was typeset in Balsamiq Sans, Kidprint MT and Roger
The illustrations were prepared with hand-carved stamps and digital techniques

Hardback ISBN 978-1-64686-289-4
Paperback ISBN 978-1-64686-424-9
Paperback with enhanced CD ISBN 978-1-64686-290-0
E-book ISBN 978-1-64686-348-8

British Cataloguing-in-Publication Data:
a catalogue record for this book is available from the British Library

Library of Congress Cataloging-in-Publication Data
is available under LCCN 2021015451

1 3 5 7 9 8 6 4 2

Go to *www.barefootbooks.com/yogaadventure* to access
your audio singalong and video animation online.

Barefoot Books

step inside a story

At Barefoot Books, we celebrate art and story that opens the hearts and minds of children from all walks of life, focusing on themes that encourage independence of spirit, enthusiasm for learning and respect for the world's diversity. The welfare of our children is dependent on the welfare of the planet, so we source paper from sustainably managed forests and constantly strive to reduce our environmental impact. Playful, beautiful and created to last a lifetime, our products combine the best of the present with the best of the past to educate our children as the caretakers of tomorrow.

www.barefootbooks.com

After teaching preschool for almost 8 years, **Jamaica Stevens** founded JAMaROO Kids in 2004, specializing in providing music, dance and yoga classes for young children. Jamaica and her team teach weekly classes, produce original music and create curriculum for their students. She lives in San Francisco, California, USA. Learn more at *JAMaROOKids.com*.

Rocío Alejandro has illustrated many children's books published both in her home country of Argentina and abroad. In 2017, she won the X Compostela Prize for her book *Simon's Vegetable Garden*. She has also illustrated the Mindful Tots series for Barefoot Books.